KISS! KISS! YUCK! YUCK!

Story by

Kyle Mewburn

Illustrations by

Ali Teo & John O'Reilly

PEACHTREE

ATLANTA

Auntie Elsie was always pleased to see Andy.

"Hi-de-hi,
Andy Apple Pie!"

she yelled.

But Andy was too slow.

Auntie Elsie's arms **swooped out**
and grabbed him in a squishy hug.

Andy wriggled.

He held his breath.

But the sloppy kisses came, all the same.

KISS! KISS!
on the left cheek.

KISS!

KISS!
on the right cheek.

YUCK!
YUCK!
Andy said to himself.

The next time Auntie Elsie came to visit, Andy hid under his bed.

"Where's my **Andy Apple Jelly?**"
cried Auntie Elsie.

He lay as still as a **stone.**

KEEP OUT!
BY ORDER OF: Andy

"Oh my!"
said Auntie Elsie.

"Look at this **toy truck,**
driving by itself."

What **toy truck?**

Andy just had to have a peek.

"There you are! What a **surprise!**"

cried Auntie Elsie as she grabbed him.

Andy
squirmed.

He shut his eyes.

But the sloppy kisses came,
all the same.

KISS! KISS!
on the left cheek.

KISS! KISS!
on the right cheek.

YUCK! YUCK!
Andy said to himself.

The next time,
Andy hid in the chicken house
under a pile of straw.

Auntie Elsie came up the path,
stomp, stomp,

and opened the door,
squeak, squeak.

"Oh my!"
said Auntie Elsie.

"This **chicken** has laid an **egg**
as big as a football."

Andy lifted his head
to look.

Rats!
He'd been tricked again.

"Got you,
Andy Apple Sauce!"

yelled Auntie Elsie,
picking him up.

Andy grumped and grizzled
but the sloppy kisses came, all the same.

**KISS!
KISS!**

on the left cheek.

**KISS!
KISS!**

on the right cheek.

"You taste
like feathers,"

said Auntie Elsie.

Every time Auntie Elsie came,

Andy tried to hide.

Every time, she found him
and gave him

sloppy kisses.

When he climbed a tree,

she
climbed
up after him.

KISS!
KISS!

KISS!
KISS!

When he hid in the pig pen, she climbed over the fence.

She didn't mind the pigs
and she didn't mind the mud.

"Howdy-dumble,

Andy Apple Crumble!" she yelled.

"Where's MY HUG?"

Muddy **kiss** on the left cheek!

Muddy **kiss** on the right cheek!

YUCK!

went Andy.

OINK!

went the pigs.

The next week,

Andy crawled under the house
among the **spiderwebs.**

Auntie Elsie
didn't like

spiders.

He waited and waited all afternoon,
but Auntie Elsie never came.

"Where's Auntie Elsie?"
Andy asked.

"She fell off a **camel** in Australia,"
said his father.

"Poor Elsie.
She broke her leg."

Auntie Elsie didn't come the next week,
or the next,
or the next.

The **chickens** laid their eggs,

the **pigs** oinked their oinks,

and Andy **waited** at the window.

No Auntie Elsie!

One day, a taxi stopped by the gate.
The door opened.

Out came **two crutches,**

a **leg** in a **cast,**

and then...

"AUNTIE ELSIE!"

yelled Andy.

He flew through the house,
along the path,
and down to the gate!

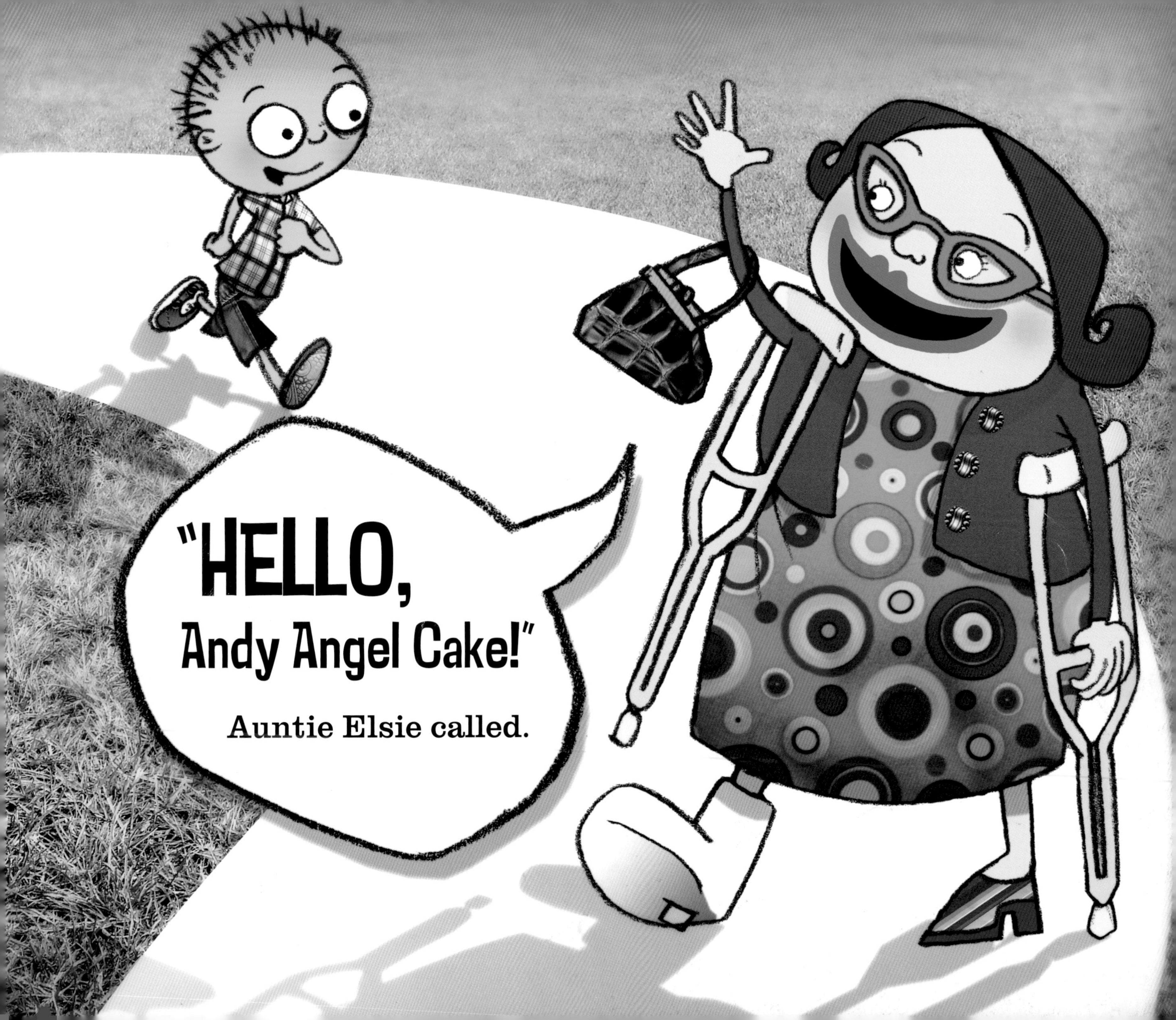
"HELLO,
Andy Angel Cake!"
Auntie Elsie called.

Andy's arms swooped out.
He grabbed Auntie Elsie
and gave her two big, sloppy kisses.

He kissed her
on the left cheek.

He kissed her
on the right cheek.

KISS!
KISS!
HUG! HUG!

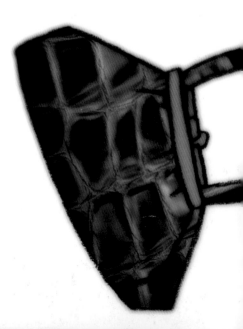

Published by
PEACHTREE PUBLISHERS
1700 Chattahoochee Avenue
Atlanta, Georgia 30318-2112
www.peachtree-online.com

First published in New Zealand in 2006 by Scholastic New Zealand Limited
First United States edition published in 2008 by Peachtree Publishers

Book design by Ali Teo and John O'Reilly
Illustrations created in pencil, collage, and digital treatment

Printed in Singapore
10 9 8 7 6 5 4 3 2 1
First Edition

ISBN 13: 978-1-56145-457-0 / ISBN 10: 1-56145-457-5

Cataloging-in-Publication Data is available from the Library of Congress